The Iceberg Express

David Cory

The Iceberg Express

The Magic Comb

One bright morning in August little Mary Louise put on her hat and went trudging across the meadow to the beach.

It was the first time she had been trusted out alone since the family had moved to the seashore for the summer; for Mary Louise was a little girl, nothing about her was large, except her round gray eyes.

There was a pale mist on the far-off sea, and up around the sun were white clouds edged with the hues of pinks and violets. The tide was coming in, and the waves, little at first, but growing larger every moment, were crowding up, along the sand and pebbles, laughing, winking and whispering, as they tumbled over each other, like thousands of children hurrying home from school.

Who was down there under the blue water, with the hoarse, hollow voice, urging and pushing them across the beach to her feet? And what was there beneath the sea, and beyond the sea, so deep, so broad and so dim, away off where the white ships, that looked smaller than seabirds, were gliding out and in?

But while Mary Louise stood still and wondered, there came a low rippling laugh to her ear.

A little distance down the beach a girl, somewhat older than herself, rested on the beach. She evidently was tired from swimming, for she lay half in the water and half on the warm sand, her face resting on her upturned palms, looking at Mary Louise with a smile, which seemed to say: "Why don't you come over and comb my hair?"

Indeed, this must have been exactly what she meant, for she held out a pretty pearl comb until Mary Louise could resist no longer.

Little Mary Louise had never before seen such beautiful long hair. It spread like a scarf from the girl's shoulders down upon the sand.

Mary Louise had forgotten that there were mermaids, and that mermaids always had most beautiful hair, and that they always combed it with pearly combs!

"Have you been swimming?" asked Mary Louise.

"Yes, a long swim," answered the little mermaid, and she gave a sudden kick in the water with her little feet, or, should I say, with her small fin-tail, which sent the spray flying.

"Oh, you're a mermaid!" exclaimed Mary Louise, surprised and delighted at her unexpected discovery. "I saw your finny tail. Do you like tails better than feet?"

"I never had feet," said the little mermaid, "so I can't say, but I should think they'd be very nice to walk on."

"Yes, if you go to the mountains, as we did last summer," answered Mary Louise, "but you don't have to climb hills in the ocean."

"Perhaps you don't know there are mountains in the sea," said the little mermaid. "Of course, you have seen nothing but their tops. What is that little rocky ledge over yonder, where the white lighthouse stands, but the stony top of a hill rising from the bottom of the sea? And what are those pretty green islands, with their clusters of trees and grassy slopes, but the summits of hills lifted out of the water?"

"Oh!" said Mary Louise, with a gasp. "You do know geography, don't you? Is it pretty, away down there under the waves?" she added wistfully.

The mermaid smiled very sweetly as she answered, "Yes, it is. There are many wonderful things to see, and many strange beautiful things to hear under the sea! I will comb your hair with my magic comb," and she ran the pearly comb gently through Mary Louise's hair.

"Over the sea the white ships sail,

Out through the mist and the rollicking gale,

While deep below the mermaids swim

With their finny tails so neat and trim.

So please, little magic comb, don't fail

To give Mary Louise a mermaid tail."

And the more she combed the longer grew the pretty curls, until, to the astonishment of Mary Louise, she found her hair trailing down to her very feet. The breeze suddenly blew it to one side, and there on the sand, instead of her two little shoes, was a mermaid's tail, with a flippy-floppy fin on the end!

"Come with me," said the mermaid, and without a moment's hesitation Mary Louise followed her into the water and out beyond the breakers, swimming as easily as if she had always been a little mermaid, instead of a girl who wore tan shoes.

"Where are we going?" asked Mary Louise, as the dim line of the shore disappeared and there was nothing in sight but the great, restless ocean.

The mermaid did not answer, but looked about intently, as if trying to find something.

"What are you looking for?" asked Mary Louise, for she was a curious little girl, and forgot one question as soon as she asked another.

"Oh, there it is!" exclaimed the mermaid. "Come with me. Hold your hands out before you like this and dive down!"

"But where are we going?" again asked Mary Louise as they sank lower and lower in the sea.

"Oh, I forgot," answered the mermaid, turning with a smile to her little companion; "I was so busy looking for the subway entrance that I forgot your question."

"Goodness!" cried Mary Louise. "I didn't know there was a subway in the sea!"

"To be sure," answered the mermaid. "The track lies along the bottom of the ocean. It's not a railroad train we're going to take, but a water train that comes all the way from the Northern seas, sweeping on like a river in the sea. Wait till we get down there. You'll see how fast it goes."

Mary Louise was too astonished to speak.

"The Pullman cars," continued the mermaid, "are icebergs. They come from the North every summer to take a trip South."

"Whew!" shivered Mary Louise. "I think we ar near one now, for I feel quite cold."

Sure enough, she was right, for there close at hand was a great white object.

"All aboard!" shouted a big polar bear. "Watch your step!"

The mermaid helped Mary Louise to slide on a projecting ledge, and off they went.

"Now we can enjoy the scenery," laughed the mermaid, as she arranged her tail in an artistic curve and brushed back her hair, which had been swept over her eyes by the swift action of the water.

"The train never stops, you know, until it reaches its destination, but that need not interfere with our getting off any time we please should you wish to visit any pretty spot we pass on our journey."

Just at that moment there was a tremendous crash and Mary Louise found herself thrown off into the water, while a muffled roar rolled through the depths of the ocean.

The Coral Palace

"Why, the ocean is full of cracked ice!" exclaimed Mary Louise, as she and the mermaid rose to the surface and looked about them. "I wonder what it was that caused such a tremendous crash?"

"Perhaps the Whale Ice Trust is after a big ice supply," replied the mermaid with a laugh. "The ocean depths are no longer a quiet place since this dreadful hot weather set in. Just the other day I heard the King of the Mermen say that they were about to send a note of protest to Neptune for violating the laws of Merland!"

"I don't know much about it," said Mary Louise, "except that it's very inconvenient to have one's voyage disturbed in such a way. What are we going to do now?"

"How would you like to visit the Court of the Mer King?" asked the mermaid.

"Oh, lovely!" cried Mary Louise. "I've never met any kinds, although I've read about them in fairy stories."

"Come along then," said the mermaid. "Follow me straight down, for I think we are not very far from the Coral Palace, where King Seaphus holds court."

Placing the palms of her hands together diving fashion, she gave her pretty tail a kick-off, and away she went, head downward, through the water.

Mary Louise followed her example, somewhat surprised at the ease with which she executed this difficult maneuver.

In a short time they found themselves on the bottom of the ocean. In the distance could be seen the dim outline of a magnificent castle of pink and white coral. Leading up to it was a wide highway, flanked on either side with beautiful sea-grass, and dotted here and there, like milestones, stood columns of beautiful coral. Banks of exquisite mother-of-pearl rose at intervals along the way; water plants of various hues grew in wild profusion.

"Why, it's very much like the earth," exclaimed Mary Louise, "only one doesn't walk, and its not dusty, and — and it's not hot and sunny!"

"No, indeed!" said the mermaid. "But sometimes we have a pest of water gnats that are worse than mosquitoes, and we have to put up netting on our bedroom windows to keep them out."

As she finished speaking they approached the door of the castle, on which she knocked with a flap of her finny tail. It was immediately opened by a merman dressed in the uniform of a court page. "What can I do for you, Your Highness?" he asked, bowing low.

"Why, are you a princess?" asked Mary Louise in surprise, turning quickly to the mermaid and forgetting for the moment that they were on the steps of a real merman's castle.

The little mermaid only laughed in reply, and taking Mary Louise by the hand led her through the coral doors to King Seaphus.

His Majesty was seated on a throne of pearl, studded with many precious stones. A long emerald robe fell from his shoulders and on his head rested a magnificent crown set with glittering jewels, which gleamed and sparkled in the dim light of the royal chamber.

"Ah, my daughter, whom have you here?" he asked, leaning from the throne and gazing intently at little Mary Louise. "Methinks she is a mermaidized mortal!" At which the King laughed loudly, for he was very fond of coining words and was busily engaged, when his state duties did not interfere, in compiling a new dictionary.

"You are right, Father Seaphus," replied his beautiful daughter. "Let me introduce little Mary Louise."

The King rose graciously and extended his royal right hand. Mary Louise made a low curtsey, finding it much easier now that she was a mermaid to perform this little act of graciousness on account of the flexibility of her tail.

Legs, of course, are indispensable for walking; but, then, in these days of new inventions, when the air is invaded by wing, and the earth traversed by wheels, and the depths of the waters by mechanical fins, walking may soon become a lost art! Something like this may have flitted through her mind, but she only answered in a trembling voice, "How do you do, Your Majesty!"

"You are welcome, 'Mermaid Mary,' to our Kingdom of the Sea," he replied. "I hope you will enjoy your stay with us." So saying, he gallantly lifted his gold crown as little Mary Louise made another curtsey.

"Let us dress for dinner," said the mermaid.

They swam quickly upstairs between two balustrades of lovely coral to her bedroom.

It was just like fairy-land; at least, it seemed so to little Mary Louise, as she looked about the pretty room. In one corner stood a beautiful bed of mother-of-pearl, hung with varied colored sea grass for curtains. Sea moss made it as soft as down. In fact, it seemed almost softer to Mary Louise, who by this time was very sleepy. She rested her tired little body upon the cushions and in a few short seconds was sound asleep. The princess mermaid looked at her with loving eyes, while she sang very low and sweetly:

"Sleep, little sister, for when you awake,

We'll have a fine dinner of fishes and cake!"

I think the mermaid took somewhat after her royal father for she often spoke in rhyme, which she composed as she talked, while his great delight, as has been mentioned before, was to coin a new word for his dictionary.

Leaving Mary Louise to her slumbers, the princess mermaid sat herself down before her mirror and combed her hair. Presently, she went over to her wardrobe and took out a beautiful shimmery pink shawl. What it was made of I cannot tell, except that it shivered and quivered with little colors like a rainbow. Perhaps it was made of changeable sea-silk.

At any rate, Mary Louise, who at that moment opened her eyes, thought it was the most exquisite thing she had ever seen.

"Is it really for me? Is it really?" she asked with a cry of delight, as the mermaid came toward her.

"Of course it is, my dear," replied the mermaid princess, "and as soon as you have put it on, and combed your hair—you needn't wash your hands and face, you know—the banquet will be ready."

Mary Louise clapped her hands and hopped, or, rather, flopped about, so happy was she to receive such a gift in the depths of the sea.

When she was dressed in the lovely shawl, and a beautiful mother-of-pearl comb fastened in her hair, the princess mermaid declared she looked "too sweet for anything!" Then they floated down, arm in arm, to the great dining hall.

King Seaphus

The great dining hall of King Seaphus was considered by all the inhabitants of Merland—that is, all those who had been lucky enough to have seen its splendor—to be the most magnificent of its kind anywhere.

The dining table, or banquet board, as it was called, was made of mother-of-pearl. The pale, shimmery cloth was woven from the most delicate of sea-grasses. The gold and silver plates shone with a strange luster, and the goblets, fashioned of the thinnest and most exquisite pearl, gave the impression that they were strange sea lilies.

King Seaphus seated himself majestically at the head of the banquet board, and little Mary Louise was shown the place on his right. At the other end sat the Mermaid Princess. Mermen in dark green liveries served the meal. But what delighted and interested Mary Louise the most was the way in which the food was served. Instead of ordinary, everyday dishes, it appeared in little airtight boats, which the servants guided dexterously to the table, and when opened, the steam escaped in hundreds of little bubbles that took on all the hues of the rainbow. These slowly ascended through the pale green water until they reached the surface, where they probably floated off in the air, until they burst, like fairy soap-bubbles.

All kinds of delicious fish, little pink and white crabs, goldfish, luscious oysters, and, finally, coral-candy, made up the different courses of the dinner. When it was over and the coffee was served in a beautiful room adjoining, King Seaphus smoked a big cigar, which, to Mary Louise's amazement, glowed and burned like any ordinary Havana her father smoked at home.

After King Seaphus had smoked away in perfect silence for some time, he turned to Mary Louise and asked:

"Where were you going, my dear, when you met my daughter?"

"Oh, nowhere in particular," replied little Mary Louise quickly. "You see, I was playing on the beach when I saw the Princess, and—and—and—-"

"Then I combed her hair with my magic comb," said the Princess, coming to the relief of little Mary Louise, who was very much embarrassed by the question. You see, she was not at all accustomed to hold conversation with royalty, and to be talking to a Merman King was, perhaps, even more disconcerting.

"We took the subway," continued his daughter, "we caught the Iceberg Express, and, well, here we are."

"So I see," said the King.

Mary Louise gave a giggle and, forgetting her embarrassment, exclaimed, "And just as we were safe on board, after the Polar Bear porter had told us to 'watch our step,' there was an awful explosion, and we found ourselves floating about in the midst of a lot of cracked ice."

"Indeed," exclaimed King Seaphus, "this is the second time in the last month we've had an accident on the Sea Bottom Subway. I must call in my Prime Minister and have an investigation begun at once."

Pulling vigorously on a beautifully braided sea-grass rope, he awaited the coming of a page. Little Mary Louise heard the far-off tinkle of the bell, and presently the Mer-bell-boy appeared.

"Summon his most excellent self, the Prime Minister," commanded King Seaphus.

The Mer-boy page glided away and presently appeared, deferentially escorting the Prime Minister. The latter was a very distinguished looking person. His long, white beard was parted gracefully in the center, no doubt by the action of the water as he swam up to where the King sat. As befitted so important an official, he was clad in a long, red robe, which reached nearly to the end of his fin-tail. His head was adorned with a crimson cap and tassel made of the softest velvet sea-grass.

"What is your majesty's command?" he asked, bending low before King Seaphus. The King did not reply for a moment. He was a wise King, and thought for several minutes before he spoke. This made the Prime Minister fidget about on his tail. If he had been a Prime Minister of any land, and not of the sea, he probably would have stood first on one leg and then on the other, but, as he had no feet, he shifted about uneasily on his fin-tail until the King spoke.

"I hear there has been another wreck on the Sea Bottom Subway."

The Prime Minister coughed, and little bubbles rose from the end of his nose, the sight of which almost caused Mary Louise to giggle aloud. But she remembered her manners in time and saved herself the mortification of such a breach of etiquette.

"Yes, Your Royal Highness," admitted the Prime Minister, "but I understand it was not at all serious. One of the Iceberg cars was demolished, and one of the Polar Bear porters, I believe, although I am not certain at the moment, was slightly injured. None of the passengers was hurt, with the possible exception of a Star Fish, who complained of a slight pain in one of his five fingers — I forget, for the moment, which finger."

"Is the road again in operation?" inquired King Seaphus.

"Not yet, your Royal Highness," replied the Prime Minister, "but I have every assurance from the management that trains will be running, at the very latest, by tomorrow morning."

"You will have to spend the night with us, then," said the Princess, turning to Mary Louise, with a smile. "You know," she added in a whisper, "I'm glad there was an accident; otherwise you would not have come to our castle, and we might not have grown to be such friends."

"Don't whisper, my daughter," said King Seaphus. "Your mother will think, should she hear that you had been so rude during her absence, that she cannot leave home to even visit her mother for a week without your becoming demoralized."

The Prime Minister coughed behind his hand, while the little bubbles rose again through the pale green of the sea-water. Mary Louise felt quite embarrassed, and the little Princess blushed. King Seaphus looked sternly at all three.

Just then a loud knocking was heard on the castle door. "Billows and breakers!" exclaimed the King, "what is that?"

King Seaphus waited anxiously as the knocking on the castle door continued. "Billows and breakers," he exclaimed again, expectantly waiting for the visitor or visitors to be announced.

Just as his impatience was nearly exhausted, a court page appeared escorting a Polar Bear and a Star Fish. Mary Louise at once recognized the former as the porter on the Iceberg Express. The visitors bowed respectfully to the King, and the little Star Fish winked one of his five small eyes at the Princess. The Polar Bear smiled at Mary Louise, but said nothing.

"Well," exclaimed King Seaphus, after a brief silence, "you honor us by your presence, but, what do you want?"

"I want redress," cried the Star Fish in a queer little gurgle.

"You want what?" thundered the King, realizing now that his visitors were looking for damages on account of the accident. This naturally worried him, as he was a heavy stockholder in the Sea Bottom Subway.

"One of my five fingers has been badly bruised," continued the Star Fish, "for which reason I shall sue for damages."

"I have suffered internal injuries," said the Polar Bear, speaking up quickly, encouraged by the independent manner of the Star Fish.

"Internal injuries!" laughed the King; "infernal fiddlesticks, I have heard that tune before!"

"Your Highness," interposed the Star Fish, "my condition is quite serious. As I have but five fingers, to have one of them injured is far worse than to have one of my feet, for of the latter I have hundreds."

The King looked at him inquiringly. Although he was Monarch of the Sea, perhaps he did not know that a Star Fish, while he has hundreds of little feet, has no legs at all. Even his feet do not move as ordinary feet do, one before the other; they can only cling like little suckers pulling him slowly along from place to place.

"Neither am I like the everyday common fish. My mouth is in the center of my body, and I have a little scarlet-colored sieve through which I strain the sea-water. I couldn't think of swallowing sea-water with everything that might be floating in it."

"Holy mackerel!" exclaimed the King, under his breath, "I'd better settle with this individual as quickly as possible. He'll drive me crazy if I don't, and maybe, cause me no end of trouble."

"Your Royal Highness," began the Polar Bear, "I was hit by a large piece of ice in the chest."

"In the ice-chest or in the ice-box?" inquired the King, his humor getting the better of his anger, for he could never let go by an opportunity to make a pun.

"Your Royal Highness," interrupted the Star Fish, "I wish to state that I took this little trip for my health. My doctor told me I must go South. So I boarded the Iceberg Express at Cape Cod, intending to spend the summer in the mountains."

"In the mountains!" roared King Seaphus. "You don't go to the seashore for the mountains! You should have gone inland to the White Mountains or the Catskills—those are well-known summer resorts."

"May it please your Royal Highness," said the Star Fish, stroking his beautiful purple coat with one of his five little fingers, "I was bound for the Caribbean Sea, which is as full of mountains as New Hampshire and Vermont are. Of course, none of them have caps of snow like Mount Washington, for it's nice and warm in the Caribbean Sea; that's the reason I want to go there. But, if the Iceberg Express is wrecked, how am I to continue my journey?"

"Sufferin' mackerel!" exclaimed King Seaphus; this time he uttered the words aloud and not under his breath, "Sufferin' mackerel! I'll see that you get there, if I have to charter a special train!"

"But what about my finger?" asked the Star Fish.

"Oh, I'll reimburse you for your ticket," exclaimed the King. "And now, what can I do for you?" he asked, turning to the Polar Bear.

"Train Porters have very low wages," replied the Polar Bear.

"Very well," answered King Seaphus, "I will see that yours are doubled," and he waved the two visitors away with a haughty gesture. The court page then escorted them to the door.

"You heard what I said," cried the King, turning to the Prime Minister. "Now go to the General Manager of the Sea Bottom Subway and inform him of my wishes. Also that he must have an express ready to start for the Caribbean Sea tomorrow morning without fail."

The Prime Minister bowed respectfully and departed.

"Whew!" exclaimed the King, smiling at Mary Louise and his daughter as soon as the three were again alone, "if that Star Fish wasn't a walking encyclopedia! He had everything at his five finger-ends!"

"I think I'll take the same train as the little Star Fish," said Mary Louise, "for I've never been to the Caribbean Sea and I think it must be a lovely place."

"May I go with Mary Louise?" asked the Mermaid Princess.

"Well, I don't see why not," answered her father, after a pause, "only you must get back inside of a fortnight, for your mother will be home by that time."

"I must see that my mother-of-pearl trunk is packed," said the Princess. "Come with me, Mary Louise." Then curtseying to the King, they swam up the water stairway to the room of the little mermaid.

The next morning found Mary Louise and the Mermaid Princess waiting anxiously at the station for the Iceberg Express. On the platform they recognized among the passengers their little friend, the Star Fish. In a few minutes the express thundered into the station. "Watch your step!" yelled the Polar Bear Porter as he helped Mary Louise and the Princess on board. Then with a rush and a roar the Iceberg Express started on its journey for the Mountains of the Sea!

The Wreck

Mary Louise and the Mermaid Princess settled themselves back comfortably in their seats and looked about them. The Iceberg Express certainly had every convenience. Of course almost everything was made of ice. But, then, so is most everything in a Pullman car made of steel. There was really very little difference except that the ice was much prettier, it was so clear and white, and the moss cushions that covered the seats were soft and springy. The crystal chandeliers that hung from the ceiling were resplendent with little twinkling lights, and the curtains at the ice-paned windows were made of the thinnest spun ice threads. Even the little drinking cups that were packed in a column, one within the other, at the ice water tank, were made of thin ice.

"I don't feel the least bit cold," said Mary Louise, turning with a laugh to her mermaid friend. "Do you?"

"Not the least bit," she replied.

"It's so different, though, from the first train we were on," continued Mary Louise. "It isn't anything like it really. Why, the first train was only an ordinary iceberg, don't you remember?"

"That's because we never went inside," replied the mermaid. "We didn't have the opportunity, the explosion came so soon."

"That's so," agreed Mary Louise. "The only think I distinctly remember is the Polar Bear porter calling out to be careful, and then the awful explosion. After that we were in the water and there was nothing around us but cracked ice."

"Dining car in the rear," announced the Polar Bear porter, walking down the isle with a menu card held gracefully in his paw. "Last call for the dining car!"

"Goodness!" exclaimed Mary Louise. "Let's hurry, or we won't be able to get anything to eat, and I always love to eat in a dining car."

Jumping up from the seat, she and the Princess swam down the aisle, across the vestibuled platform, through the next car, and then into the diner.

There were quite a number of passengers still seated at the different little tables. A soldierly looking Penguin sat at one and a few tables beyond a motherly looking Seal with a baby boy Seal at her side was just finishing some delicious looking pink water ice.

Mary Louise and the Mermaid sat down at the nearest table and looked over the menu. It was great fun selecting what they wanted, and when they had finished their water ices they felt that they had dined most sumptuously.

They then returned to their seats and looked out of the window for a time. Strange sights met their eyes as the train rushed on. There were no telegraph poles to count, nor cows to see grazing in green meadows. Instead, however, were numerous fish swimming here and there, some of gorgeous coloring, others of white or silver hue. Hills and valleys of sand, as well as long meadows of seaweed, stretched away for miles and miles. Strange-looking sea animals crawled close to the rushing train. If they came too close the suction of the water drew them along until they disappeared beneath the car.

As darkness settled down over the quiet deep, Mary Louise turned from the window with a sigh. "I feel sleepy already," she said, "and it's only supper time!"

"We'll tell the porter to make up our berths," said the Mermaid Princess. "He can do it while we are having our supper in the dining car."

On their return they found their berth in readiness. Soft green seaweed curtains hung gracefully to the floor, one of them being drawn aside, showing a little white bed. It looked as comfortable as her own little bed at home, Mary Louise thought.

It took the two little mermaids but a few minutes to undress, and as soon as their tired heads touched the pillow they were sound asleep.

Softly the seabells are ringing away,

Dipping and dripping and white with the spray,

Ding-dong, and ding-dong, and ding-dong, so deep,

The seabells are singing me softly to sleep.

Over and over again in her dreams little Mary Louise repeated this song. Then suddenly the bells seemed to change their tune. They clanged out wildly until a sudden loud crash awoke her with a start. The engine whistle was sending forth loud, warning cries. The Mermaid Princess began to tremble with fright.

"What do you suppose is the matter?" she whispered.

"I'm sure I don't know," replied little Mary Louise. "Perhaps there's something on the track."

By this time all the passengers were thrusting their heads out through the curtains of their berths.

"Porter, Porter!" called the Penguin, who had been vainly pressing the electric call-button.

But as usual, when a porter was wanted he is nowhere to be found.

Then the Baby Seal began to cry. Suddenly all the lights went out. Mary Louise hastily caught up her clothes and commenced dressing. "Thank goodness," she said in a trembling voice, "I don't have to bother with stockings!"

"I never was anything but a Mermaid," said the Princess in a frightened whisper, "so I don't know anything about them!"

"Where's my waist?" asked Mary Louise, hardly able to keep from crying. "I can't find it anywhere, and it's so dreadfully dark, too."

"Oh, dear me!" suddenly cried the Mermaid Princess. "I believe I'm trying to get yours on over mine. I'm so excited I forgot that I already had on my own."

"Well, I'm dressed at last," exclaimed Mary Louise after wriggling and squirming about for a few minutes longer. "Isn't it awful hard work dressing in a berth?"

Suddenly the engine bell clanged out more furiously than ever. The whistle shrieked again and again. Mary Louise looked with frightened eyes at the princess who gave a cry of terror and threw her arms about her neck as the lights again went out. Then there was a sudden crash, and the Iceberg Express shivered and toppled over.

The next instant Mary Louise and the Mermaid Princess found themselves in the water.

It was quite warm and pleasant, and in a few minutes they reached the surface. To their surprise they saw their fellow passenger, the little Star Fish, swimming near them, and not far away, on a piece of ice, the Polar Bear porter.

"Where are we?" asked Mary Louise. But no one replied to her question, although the Star Fish looked all around, before and behind and both sides at once, which I'm sure you can't do no matter how hard you may try — while with his fifth eye he kept a bright lookout for sharks.

Presently the Polar Bear porter replied, "I think we are in the Caribbean Sea."

And if you don't know where that is, please get out you map of North America, although school is over, and find it.

"I never thought we'd get here so soon," said the little Star Fish at last. "You see, I boarded the train somewhere off Cape Cod. And that's a long way from here."

"I got on much farther north," said the Polar Bear porter, fanning himself with a large sea shell. "Gracious me, but it's dreadfully hot down here."

"This Caribbean Sea is as full of mountains as New Hampshire and Vermont are, but none of them have caps of snow like that which Mount Washington sometimes wears," said the Mermaid Princess. "Snow wouldn't last a second under this hot sun."

"Where did you learn all this?" asked Mary Louise.

"Oh, I went to the Coral School for Girls," answered the Mermaid Princess, and she sighed, for she suddenly remembered she was a long way from home.

Just then the little Star Fish met a soft little body, much smaller than himself, who invited him to visit her relatives, who live, by millions, in this mountain region.

So off they started for Coraltown, where this little Miss Polyp lived.

Her father and mother, brothers and sisters, uncles and aunts, were all polyps. They had built the coral islands by fastening themselves to the tops of the mountains under the sea, year after year, and at last their soft bodies had turned into stone. And now you know how these millions of little polyps finally made the small islands that dotted the surface of the water.

After the Star Fish and his little friend had swum away, Mary Louise spied a boat drifting toward them. So she and the Mermaid Princess scrambled inside, and the polar Bear porter hoisted a sail, which he found wrapped around a mast in the bottom of the boat.

"Hip, hurrah, we're off once more,"

Shouted the Polar Bear, waving his paw,

And the Mermaid Princess laughed in glee

As he held the tiller and sailed o'er the sea!

By and by the air became colder and the Mermaid said:

"We must be near my father's castle. I think I'll slip into the ocean and swim home."

"Before you go, please comb my hair with your magic comb so that I may be a little girl again," begged Mary Louise; "I don't want to be a mermaid forever."

As soon as the magic pearl comb touched Mary Louise's hair her tail changed into her own little pair of legs.

"Now kiss me good-by," said the little Mermaid Princess, and, with a splash, she disappeared in the ocean.

Wonderland

For a few minutes Mary Louise felt quite lonely. Presently she asked the Polar Bear to be kind enough to land her on the nearest shore.

At once the big kind animal trimmed in his sail and before long they entered a beautiful bay whose dark waters were dotted with the white sails of the fisher boats, and directly in front, climbing up to the sky, a high mountain on which stood a castle, where from a tall tower all night long shone a light that could hardly be told from the stars around it.

Mary Louise jumped from the boat to the beach, and then turned to wave good-by to the Polar Bear as he sailed away to the North Pole.

Nearby sat an old fisherman on a bench mending his net.

"Hello, little girl," he said, as Mary Louise hesitated. "Moor your little hulk 'longside o' me an' I'll spin you a yarn!"

Then he began to tell how, many hundred years ago, all the land around about was covered with a thick forest instead of the deep blue water of the bay.

Then came the great giant Cormoran, who was 18 feet high and 3 yards wide, and his wife Cormelian, who was just as big, and they brought from the hills great gray rocks which they piled up, one on the other, hundreds of feet high, until they had made a mountain. And on the top of this they built their castle, where they lived until the giant's wife died and was buried under the Chapel rock.

Then Jack the Giant Killer climbed up the mountain, and after a hard fight Cormoran was killed, and there were no more giants in the land.

Next came the Small People, who cut down most of the forest, and built cottages for themselves, ploughed the fields and made gardens.

But one day a great enchanter came that way, and his strange dress and long gray beard frightened the women and children, and they shut their doors in his face whenever he asked for a drink, for he had walked far and was tired and thirsty.

At last he found the principal man of the Small People, a little old crusty fellow and very miserly. And when the great enchanter asked him for a drink of water, the Small Man told him he didn't keep a hotel for beggars. And this made the great enchanter so angry that he struck the ground with his staff, so that it made a deep hole, and then he went upon his journey.

Soon a little spring of water bubbled up through the hole, and by and by a stream burst forth that swelled to a river, and after a time the whole land was drowned, and only the high mountain remained above the water.

But the Small People who were buried under the water didn't die. They lived on just the same, waiting for the enchanter to return and lift the spell, and the land to rise, again with all the people on it.

When the old fisherman had finished his story, he said, "I will take you in my boat to see the Small People deep down in the water.

"Yes, come with me in my boat and you shall see the Wonderland under the Sea."

As soon as the old fisherman had hoisted the sail, away they went out to sea over a wide path of moonlight like a silver road leading straight out to the sky where it dipped down to the water.

All of a sudden Mary Louise noticed something come close up under the side of the boat, and remain there staring straight at her. She bent over until she nearly touched the water, when what she had taken for a fish appeared to be a very odd-looking little man. He was even shorter than she, very broad about the shoulders, with funny little arms and feet that were brought together at the heels, with the toes turned straight out when he stood up, making them look like a fish's tail. His eyes were big and round, without any eyelids or eyebrows. But his mouth was the funniest part, and when he opened it, he looked like a fish trying to talk. He was dressed in silvery white, shaded to blue and green.

With a sudden nod, he pointed to the road which opened behind him down through the depths of the water until lost in the distance.

Little Mary Louise could not take her eyes from him, and, forgetting all about the old fisherman and the boat, she bent over more and more, so as to look closer at the funny little old man, until, splash! down she went into the water.

Then came a tremendous ringing in her ears and she felt her breath go and she knew nothing more until she found herself standing with the strange little fish man by the side of a splendid carriage made of a scallop shell, burnished until it shone with pearl and silver, and drawn by two beautiful gold-fish and two silver-fish harnessed with the silken threads of the finest sea-mosses, and driven by an old coachman that looked like a mackerel.

"We are the sea-horses of the deep,

And we race through the waters blue,

Faster than wind and swifter than tide

We gallop the ocean through."

"Jump in," said the little old fish man; and without a question Mary Louise stepped into the carriage and sat down on the beautiful pea-green cushions.

Then the little man got in, the mackerel-faced coachman cracked his whip, the gold and the silver fishes darted ahead, and away they went.

Great trees waved their long branches as the carriage swept past, and odd-looking shapes came out from behind them. Huge mouths opened and shut, long arms waved about trying to catch anything in their reach, and fierce looking monsters with fishes' heads came rushing in from all sides, to stare at little Mary Louise with their great savage eyes.

Presently the little old man stood up and bowing politely, told them that Mary Louise had never caught a fish with a cruel hook.

Then these dreadful monsters snapped their horny jaws and swam away.

At once the mackerel-faced coachman whipped up his team of gold and silver fishes and away they went spinning down the road again.

At last the carriage stopped in front of a fine mansion, and Mary Louise and the little old man jumped out on the smooth beach of sparkling sand which sloped down to a glassy lake on which curious and beautiful little boats were sailing in all directions.

Along the edge of the lake were many houses, some stately castles and some little cottages. The little cottages were covered with creeping plants abloom with red flowers and the stately castles with moss like vines.

But the people. Oh dear me! They were the strangest folk! Some had very long noses and ugly looking teeth in their wide mouths, and others were so thin they looked like small sticks, and others so round that they could almost trundle themselves along like a coach-wheel. Some were dressed in the shabbiest clothes, others in splendid suits, and some covered with knobs and spikes and strange looking armor.

"Come," said the little fish man, and he led Mary Louise into his house.

Presently he brought out from a closet a quaintly shaped box. "It is the legend of Wonderland that a little girl shall break the spell that hangs over us. For it is deemed well-nigh impossible that a mortal child would venture beneath the water to visit us. Therefore, little Mary Louise, if I call all my people together, will you open this box and deliver us from the spell of the Great Enchanter?"

"I will," she answered bravely, and at once the little old fish man called together all his subjects.

As little Mary Louise looked at the box she saw printed on the cover these words:

"If a little girl mortal

    Shall uncover this prize,

The sea will sink

    And the land will rise."

And, would you believe it, the first thing she knew after carefully opening the box, she was back in the boat with the old sailor, who was shading his eyes and looking towards a beautiful green island that had suddenly come out of the water.

The Enchanted Prince

"Would you like to land on the island?" asked the old sailor who seemed in no wise surprised that an island should suddenly come up out of the sea.

"Yes," gasped little Mary Louise, "it may be a wonderful place. I certainly saw strange things beneath the water."

"To be sure you did," replied the old sailor, taking it as a matter of course that a little girl should make a trip to Wonder Land under the Sea, and return safe and sound.

But then, you know, Mary Louise may have still retained some of the charm of the little mermaid's magic comb.

Well, anyway, the old sailor steered his boat over to the green island, where Mary Louise jumped out and after saying good-by to her sailor friend, set off to look for new adventures.

After a while, she came to a great wood, where the trees were as big around as smoke stacks on an ocean liner.

All of a sudden, she heard the sound of a woodman's ax, and the crackling of the branches as they fell to the ground.

"It must be some giant cutting down a tree," she thought, and she started off in the direction of the sound, and by and by, she saw a giant beaver. He was a most wonderful sort of an animal, for he could swing an ax as well as a man. Near at hand flowed a great river, where a white water horse snorted as he dashed the spray high in the air with his forefeet.

"Are you one of Neptune's horses?" asked little Mary Louise. "I once read a story of a little boy named Hero who rode with King Neptune in his wonderful chariot."

"No, little girl," answered the beautiful sea horse kindly. "But I can show you some wonderful things. Jump on my back and I will take you to a strange place."

Then away went the great Water Horse over the water and through the spray and Mary Louise wasn't the least bit afraid although she had no water wings and might have slipped of into the water.

"Where are we going?" she asked, after a while, for by this time they were far away from the shore and going up a dark river.

"I'm going to show you the beautiful Green Waterfall Cave," answered the big Sea Horse, shaking his mane until it seemed almost as if it were raining.

Well, pretty soon he stopped, telling Mary Louise to bend over his back, before he swam into a big opening in a gray rock.

"Now lift up your head," he said, and when Mary Louise looked around she saw they were in a beautiful cave. All about them were strange people, Mermaids and Water Nymphs, Water Sprites and Mermen, fishes and dolphins, and even a whale, although he wasn't very large. If he had been, he wouldn't have been there, for the entrance to the cave was just wide enough for him to squeeze through.

Well, no sooner did they see the big Sea Horse, than they all said at once,

"Hail to our King!" and crowded around looking curiously at Mary Louise, and one little mermaid pinched her toe.

"This is Mary Louise," explained the great white Sea Horse. "I have brought her to our cave to see the wonders of our Water Country."

At once the whale blew a stream of water into the air, the dolphins turned somersaults and the little mermaid who had just pinched Mary Louise's toe, stood up on a big pearly shell and sang:

"In this river that leads to the sea,

We all live happy as happy can be,

The crocodile comes and opens his jaws,

And the giant crab stretches out his claws,

And the sword fish chases the sharp toothed shark,

But here we are safe when the day grows dark,

And the pale white moon looks down from the sky,

And the little star winks her golden eye."

And when she had finished, she swam up close to the big Sea Horse and picking up Mary Louise placed her in a great shell that sailed over the water just like a boat to the end of the cave where a little path ran along close to the water's edge till it came to a door.

"Tap gently three times," said the little mermaid.

And then, all of a sudden, it opened and there stood a great Sea Serpent.

"What do you want?" he asked with a dreadful hiss and his breath was like steam and his long red tongue like a thin flame.

"O wise Serpent," said the mermaid, "do not frighten little Mary Louise. She is traveling through our country and means no harm."

"Then she may come into my kingdom," replied the great Serpent, and he glided swiftly away.

"Do not fear him," said the little mermaid. "I cannot go with you, but you will be perfectly safe," and she closed the door and swam away, leaving little Mary Louise all alone.

It was a strange country in which Mary Louise found herself as she followed the great Serpent who was now some distance ahead. Great trees and moss-covered rocks were on every side, and only by keeping to the narrow path was it possible to find a way through them.

By and by the Serpent stopped at a gate in a high stone wall, which swung open slowly as he tapped upon it.

"Now, let me tell you something," he said, leading Mary Louise to a seat beneath a beautiful tree in a large garden close by a stately castle.

While she rested on the marble bench the great Serpent coiled himself in a ring, his head raised about two feet above the ground. He had wonderful black eyes and as he looked at her she almost fancied there were tears in them.

"Once upon a time, not so very long ago," he began, "a young prince lived in this castle. But one day a wicked magician disguised as a poor beggar came to the kitchen door and asked for bread. Now it happened to be baking day, and the Royal Baker had just placed a thousand loaves of dough in the oven. He was tired and hot and said to the beggar in a cross voice: 'You must wait until evening.' This made the beggar man dreadfully angry, and the next minute he waved a crooked stick above his head and cried, 'Let the master of this castle and his household become snakes!' Instantly, a great change came over all who lived in the castle. The prince turned into a serpent and all the retainers became snakes."

As he finished speaking, the poor Snake gave a low cry and hid his head in the grass.

"Cheer up," said Mary Louise, for she knew at once that the serpent was the poor prince in disguise. "I have a magic ring!"

Dear me, I forgot to mention that the Princess Mermaid had given it to little Mary Louise for a charm against evil.

"But what can that do for me?" asked the poor serpent prince.

"Leave that to me," replied little Mary Louise, and she turned the magic ring around three times, and, all of a sudden, a little Black Man appeared.

"What can I do for you, little Mistress?" he asked.

"This serpent was once a handsome prince," explained Mary Louise, "but by the magic of a wicked magician has been changed into a snake. Help him to regain his natural shape."

"That is a hard matter," said the little Black Man thoughtfully. "I know this wicked magician. He has great power and it takes a strong charm to work against his evil power."

And then the little Black Man ran his hand through his crinkly hair and thought for a while.

"There is a crimson apple that grows in the Gardens of the West," he said at last, "which if eaten, enables one to regain his natural shape. But the distance is far, and the way dangerous. And the owner of the garden refuses admittance to any man. But whether he would refuse a little girl, I do not know."

"I can but try," said little Mary Louise bravely. And when the serpent heard this, he lifted up his head and said:

"If you will undertake this great deed for me, I will give you whatever you desire, even my castle and all my lands."

"I would not take them from you," replied Mary Louise. "I am only a little girl." And she paused for a moment, wondering when and how she would return to her dear mother's home.

"How may I reach the Gardens of the West?" she asked anxiously.

"You must go down to the sea and wait for the sun to sink in the west," answered the little Black Man. "And when you see golden rays, like a bright road upon the water, call to King Neptune. I will give you a whistle made from a pearl shell on which you must blow three times, and when the King of the Sea hears it, he will come to you. But whether he will carry you across the ocean in his chariot, I know not. But you can try."

And the little Black Man disappeared.

"Do you think you will be able to do all this?" asked the serpent anxiously.

"I do," replied Mary Louise, and she opened the garden gate and made straight for the great ocean, and by and by she came to the beach, where the great waves rolled and broke into foamy spray making the pretty shells glisten in the sun.

No sooner had Mary Louise blown three times upon the magic whistle than King Neptune drove up in his beautiful chariot. His splendid horses with foamy manes raised their forefeet and snorted till the old Sea King was forced to quiet them.

"What can I do for you, pretty maiden?" he asked kindly.

"Oh please, Mr. Neptune, take me to the garden of golden apples. I must give one to a poor Snake Prince that he may regain his human form."

King Neptune remained silent for a time. At last he put his hand in his great pocket and said with a sigh:

"Here is a golden apple. It was to be a present to my wife. But it will be of greater use to this poor Snake Prince."

"Thank you, thank you," cried Mary Louise, and running hastily back to the garden she stood before the poor miserable snake.

"Here is the magic golden apple," she cried in a glad voice. No sooner had the serpent eaten the apple, than, all of a sudden, just as he swallowed the last piece, he changed into a handsome prince and all his retainers and servants who were snakes, you remember, regained their human form.

"Now you shall have whatever is in my power to grant," said the prince, "even if you ask for my castle."

"I will take nothing from you," replied generous little Mary Louise, "unless you wish to give me the ring you wear on your finger."

"It is yours," said the prince. "May you always wear it and remember me."

The Magic Seeds

Little Mary Louise placed the ring upon her finger and then bidding the Prince good-by turned her steps as she thought, towards home. But she had gone but a short way when she came to a funny little dwarf tugging at a great sunflower, and every once in a while he'd shake the stalk until down would come a shower of black seeds, which he put in a small basket.

"Hello," cried Mary Louise, "don't you want me to help you?"

When the little dwarf heard her voice, he started to run away, but Mary Louise caught him by the tail of his coat.

"Don't be afraid of me, little dwarf, I won't harm you."

So the dwarf set down his basket of seeds, and after he had straightened his coat, for it was half off his back, he said:

"I'll give you some of the seeds. They are very wonderful seeds."

Then little Mary Louise said good-by and by and by she came to a poor woodcutter's hut. In answer to her knock an old woman opened the door.

"How do you do!" she said with a bow, and then she told Mary Louise that her husband had just gone to the village for sunflower seeds. Wasn't that strange? It made Mary Louise laugh and taking from her pocket a handful she showed them to the old lady.

"My husband may not find any," she said. "Will you give me two that I may plant them on each side of our front door?" Then digging a hole in the ground on each side of the step she planted the seeds. And, would you believe it? all of a sudden a yellow stalk sprung up, and pretty soon it was as high as the door and then it was higher than the roof and before long it reached way up into the sky, so far and so high that you couldn't see the top.

"Goodness gracious me!" exclaimed the old woman. "What kind of seeds are these?"

"I'll climb up and see," and up the stalk went little Mary Louise. Bigger and bigger it grew until finally it spread out altogether into a great big meadow covered with sunflowers.

Everywhere the birds were singing and little rabbits hopping about, and nearby a flock of lambs nibbling the fresh green grass.

"Oh my!" exclaimed little Mary Louise, "this is strange, very strange!"

When, all of a sudden, one of the sunflowers began to sing:

"I love the sun in the big blue sky,

As he rolls along his pathway high,

Through the clouds and over the blue

While he brightly shines on me and you.

There's no one else that I love so much

As the golden sun with his soft warm touch."

And then all the sunflowers joined in the chorus:

"Beautiful, beautiful, beautiful sun,

We turn and follow you as you run

Over the soft and azure sky;

Beautiful sun with your golden eye."

When the song was finished, little Mary Louise went on her way, and it was very lucky for her that the grass was soft, for she wore no boots, which I forgot to mention she had left a the foot of the big giant sunflower by the side of the poor woodman's hut.

Well, by and by, she came to a little shoemaker's shop, where the shoemaker sat just outside the door.

"Have you a pair of red top boots?" she asked. And would you believe it? That shoemaker got up and walked inside his shop and took down a box from the top shelf, and there inside was a beautiful pair of red top boots, which fitted as if they had been made for her. Well wasn't that the luckiest thing that could have happened?

But perhaps it was just as lucky that she found money enough in her pocket to pay for them.

Pretty soon, not so very far, she came to a fountain where all day long the water played a soft little song:

"Over the pebbles and over the sand

I run till I reach the sea-shore land,

Where the pink shells sing and the big waves roar,

And the mermaids comb their hair on the shore."

"I think I'll follow this pretty book," said Mary Louise, "and maybe it will take me home."

She ran along its mossy banks until she came to the seashore. Right there on the soft warm sand sat a mermaid combing her long hair.

With a glad cry Mary Louise ran towards her. But it wasn't her friend the Mermaid Princess. No, she was a strange little mermaid, who gave a frightful scream and with a flop of her graceful tail, glided into the water. Just as she was about to dive down out of sight, she saw her pretty pearl comb on the beach.

"Don't be afraid of me," said Mary Louise, picking it up and leaning over the water. "I know your Princess Mermaid—daughter of King Seaphus," and she handed the little mermaid the pearly comb, who then swam away to her island of coral and pearl.

"Heigh ho," sighed little Mary Louise, "here I am by the sad sea waves with nobody to talk to," and as she had nothing to do, she dug a hole in the sand and thrusting in both her feet, covered them up. All of a sudden a tremendous crab crawled up and before she could run away, fastened his great claw in her sleeve.

"Oh I am king of the blue sea crabs,

And king of the sandy shore,

And I can fight as well as bite

With my big tre-men-dous claw.

Oh, I can pinch as well as a clam,

I'm king of all pinchers, you bet I am."

Now little Mary Louise was a brave girl, and unclasping her breastpin, she stuck the point right in the wrist of the Crab King's claw, after which he began to sing a different kind of song, and the tears came out of his eyes, and pretty soon he begged to be let alone.

"I'll give you the most beautiful pearl in all the world," he said, but Mary Louise only laughed and pointed to her torn sleeve:

"That won't mend my sleeve, King Crab. What right had you to tear it?"

"Oh, please take the pin out of my elbow," begged the tearful Crab King, so frightened that he couldn't tell whether it was his wrist or his elbow that Mary Louise was pricking. "I'll give you two pearls. Oh, please pull out your pin."

As soon as she had put away her breastpin, the Crab King started to dig in the sand and pretty soon he brought up two lovely pearls.

"But what am I to do with my torn sleeve?" asked Mary Louise, for she was still angry with that disagreeable old crab.

Without answering, the King of the Crabs crawled off into the tall sea grass and in a few minutes came back with a little package done up in sea weed, and after he had unwrapped it, what do you suppose Mary Louise saw? Why, a beautiful pale sea green coat made of sea silk. It was very beautiful and looked just like the shimmery green of the waves.

"Here is a coat of the great Crab King,

It's finer than silk or anything,

For none but a merman has ever worn

A coat so beautifully shimmery shorn,"

cried the King Crab, handing it to Mary Louise. Then he crawled away, for he wised to have the doctor see his wounded elbow, I imagine.

Candy City

Just then a little bird began to sing:

"In the valley, green and neat,

I see the print of little feet,

And way, way yonder in the glen

I see a host of little men."

"Dear me!" sighed Mary Louise. "I am too tired to walk any further."

"Jump on my back!" cried a happy voice, and up trotted a little pony named Dapple Gray.

"Oh, how nice," laughed Mary Louise, and climbing up on the saddle, rode off on this pretty little pony, and pretty soon, not so very far, they came to the place where the little men were at work. And what do you suppose they were doing. Why, you'd never guess if I gave you until the 4th of July.

They were making maple sugar out of the sap from the maple trees. First they boiled the sap in great big pots and then put it away to cool in queer little dishes of various shapes, and when the sugar hardened it was in the forms of funny little fish, queer little houses, strange animals, and, goodness knows, what not.

"Oh, we are the Sugar Candy Men,

   And we work all day in the snow

To make the maple sugar cakes

   To sell in the town below,"

sang one little man who wore a red peaked hat and long turned-up pointed shoes.

But when little Mary Louise rode up, they all stopped their work and looked at her, and the little man with the long turned up pointed shoes pulled off his red peaked cap and asked:

"What brings you here, Mary Louise? Are you fond of maple sugar candy?"

"I know lots of little boys and girls who are," answered Mary Louise with a smile.

"Well, hold open your pockets," said the little man, and he stood up on a stump alongside Dapple Gray and filled her pockets to overflowing. Wasn't that nice of him?

"You're very generous," said Mary Louise. "What can I do for you?"

"Go to yonder town and tell the dear old lady who keeps the 'Goody Sweet Tooth-Shop' that we will bring her candy tomorrow morning just as—

"The little red rooster

From his home on the hill

Sounds his merry cock-a-doo

Like a whistle shrill."

"All right," answered Mary Louise, and off she went to the little town down in the valley.

Well, by and by, after a while, and many a mile, and a song and a smile, for Mary Louise felt very happy with all those nice candies in her pocket, she came to a bridge over a river, on the other side of which nestled a little town among the trees.

Now there was a toll keeper, a funny little old lady with a crutch under her arm, at the entrance to the bridge.

"Give me a penny, Mary Louise,

For that is the toll you must pay,

If you would cross over the river to Dover,

Dover, just over the way."

sang the little old lady toll keeper.

"Here is the penny," laughed Mary Louise, leaning down from Dapple Gray and dropping it into the old lady's apron, which she help up in both hands.

"Pass on, little girl," she said, opening the gate, and in a few minutes Dapple Gray was clattering over the bridge. And pretty soon he drew up before the Goody Sweet Tooth Shop.

"I bring you good news from the little men of the glen," cried Mary Louise to the little old woman who just then looked out of the door.

"What is the news, dearie?" she asked, shading her eyes with her withered hand.

"Tomorrow morning, just at dawn,

When the little red rooster blows on his horn,

The maple sugar candy hearts,

Cute little cupids and candy darts,

In a great big box will be laid at your door

    to give to the children who come to your store."

said little Mary Louise. And how she ever could have spoken in poetry is more than I can tell, but perhaps the fairy maple sugar candy, which she had eaten on her way to town, had lent magic to her tongue.

Then the little old woman made a curtsy, and Mary Louise continued on her way, and by and by, after a while, she came to a great big bear sitting on a stone by the roadside. On the ground by his side was a big bundle tied with a thick leather strap.

Well, as soon as the bear saw Mary Louise, he took off his cap and said,

"I wish I had a pony,

    Either brown or gray,

So I could ride whate'er betide

    For many miles away."

"Why, what's the matter?" asked little Mary Louise.

"I have a splinter in my foot," answered the bear.

So Mary Louise dismounted and looked at the bear's foot, and when she found the splinter, she said:

"Now don't you cry, and don't you pout,

And I will pull the splinter out."

And would you believe it, in less than five hundred short seconds, she held the splinter under the bear's nose so he could see it, for the bear was very near sighted and couldn't even see the end of his toes.

"Dear me," sighed little Mary Louise, "I wish I were safe at home with Mother," she set out once more, and by and by she came to Candy Town.

Now I guess many a little boy and girl wonders where all the Christmas candies come from, but they wouldn't if they had once seen Peppermint City, all painted white with red stripes, just like a stick of peppermint candy.

Each house was built of white candy with columns of peppermint sticks supporting the roof. On either side the door stood lovely peppermint statues and striped pillars held up the little porches and big piazzas.

The opera house was guarded by a candy lion, and a fountain in the middle of the town spouted maple syrup. Rock candy crystal chandeliers hung from the ceilings in the rich man's house and little peppermint candlesticks made light for the workman's hut. Even the lamp posts on the corners were peppermint sticks and so were the barber poles.

"Goodness me," said Mary Louise to herself, "I wonder what would happen if it rained." But you see it never rained in Candy Country, which was mighty lucky.

"What do you wish?" asked a Chocolate Man, as she knocked on the Candy Town Gate.

The next moment the gate swung open and out marched a regiment of Lemon Soldiers dressed in Lemon Khaki Uniforms.

"Oh, I'm just lost," replied Mary Louise with a sigh.

"I'm a little traveler who goes

For miles and miles upon her toes.

But sometimes when I'm tired out

I think I hear a kind of voice shout,

'Come, ride with me upon my Goose,'

And other times it is a Moose,

And then again a steed with wings;

Or maybe some kind stranger brings

A ship that sails the ocean wide,

And so instead of walk, I ride."

"Well, well, your a little poetry maker," said the Chocolate Man. "Now you are the very person to write pretty little verses on our round peppermint candies." And then he held out his chocolate hand and drew tired Mary Louise inside the gate, after which he locked it with a silver key.

"Come with me to our Candy Factory," and he ran down the street, which was paved with little red brick candies, until he came to a big Rock Candy Building.

"Look here," gasped Mary Louise, all out of breath with running, for that Chocolate Man was the best athlete in all Peppermint City, "I said I was lost. I'm not a poetry maker. I wouldn't make poetry for anything. I want to see things, not dream about them!"

"Dear me," said the Chocolate Man, and he let go the lollypop door handle, "I'm sorry. I thought you'd like to stay here."

"Don't feel badly about it," said Mary Louise as he shook hands and said good-by. "I must find my way home. I've no time to lose."

"Heigh ho, this is a big river," she exclaimed a little later as she stood on the bank of a swiftly flowing stream.

"There isn't any bridge, how can you get across,

There isn't any boat and you haven't any horse

That could swim across this river with you upon its back,

So I guess you'll have to turn about and go back upon your track,"

sang a cross voice.

"She won't have to do anything of the sort," answered a kind voice and a little white duck in a boat rowed up to the bank.

"Come, jump aboard," quacked Commodore Drake, for that was the name of this duck sailor.

Mary Louise jumped in and away they went down the river to the deep blue sea. And after a while, maybe a mile, and perhaps a little more, they came to the restless ocean.

"Now," said the duck, with a wheezy, breezy quack, "I'll take you to the Hotel Wave Crest."

Presently they came to an island where a lovely coral building shone pinky bright in the rays of the sun. Right in front of it were two bell buoys who rang little bells to tell the man who owned the hotel that somebody wanted a room with a fresh salt water bath.

As soon as Commodore Drake had fastened the little boat to the wharf, he and Mary Louise walked up the steps and into Wave Crest Hotel.

When the proprietor, a nice old Dolphin, saw Mary Louise's lovely sea green coat, he at once asked where she had bought it.

"The King of the Crabs gave it to me."

"You don't tell me," exclaimed the old Dolphin. "Do you know that coat is a magic one?"

"What can it do?" asked Mary Louise, even more surprised than you are.

"Why, anybody who wears it can swim like a fish," answered the good-natured Dolphin. "It's better than a pair of water wings," and he turned over three times and began to sing,

"Oh, many a mile I've swum in the sea

    Like a hoop that rolls on the ground,

Over and over and over again,

Round and around and around,

But I always come right side up at last,

Out in the deep blue sea,

You bet I can do the loop de loo

High diddle diddledy dee."

As he finished speaking, the good-natured Dolphin turned a somersault, and after that I guess he thought he'd done enough to amuse Mary Louise, and the little white sailor duck, so he went inside the hotel and stood at the desk behind the big register book.

Just then a great whale came swimming by, blowing a stream of water high in the air. Maybe a piece of seaweed had tickled his nose, for when a whale spouts he's really sneezing, I'm told.

And after that a pretty Cat Fish began to purr, and I guess she would have asked Mary Louise a lot of questions if all of a sudden a Dog Fish hadn't barked, which so frightened the pussy cat fish that she went into her room and locked the door, dropping the kin in her vanity bag which she hid under her pillow.

"If you'll stay awhile," said the old Dolphin, "I'll give you the finest fish dinner you ever ate,

"A whale fish steak,

And some sea gull eggs,

And a pint of sea cow's milk,

Green sea weed sauce

And water cress

And oysters served on silk."

But, would you believe it, little Mary Louise didn't feel hungry. Instead she asked the duck sailor to take her back to the boat and to sail away, over the ocean's misty spray, until they should come to the Land of Nod where sleep is sent by the Little Dream God.

As soon as she and the little white duck reached this wonderful little land, they became sleepy and their eyes winked and blinked and pretty soon they both lay down on the soft grass and went sound to sleep. And then the twinkle, twinkle star shone down with its pretty golden eye and sang a sleepy lullaby,

"Over the ocean cool and sweet

Up to the sea grass's waving feet

Blows the wind from the rainbow west

Whispering low, 'It is time for rest.'"

Toy Land

Now, when Mary Louise and the little white sailor duck woke up in the land of Nod, they both rubbed their eyes to make sure who stood there dressed in pink pajamas and little starry crown.

It was the little Dream God. In his hand he carried a silver wand, in the handle of which was a little whistle which made a soft sound when he blew upon it.

"Did you have a good sleep?" he asked, and with a laugh, he took off his crown and sat down on the grass. And oh, what a sweet laugh it was. Just like the tinkle of a far-away bell or the ripple of a little brook.

Well, after a little talk, the big Dream Bird came out of his wicker cage and said: "I'm going to take Mary Louise for a ride," and away he flew, while the little white sailor duck went back to his boat and sailed away, too, over the ocean big and blue.

"Where would you like to go?" asked the Dream Bird. "I'm the bird who brings dreams to people. Dreams of doing great big wonderful things, you know. Not sleepy dreams."

"Take me to some place that is different from anything I've ever seen," answered Mary Louise.

So the big Dream Bird scratched his head with his foot, but for a long time he couldn't tell where to go.

Well, anyway, by and by, not so very long, for the big Dream Bird kept flying on as he scratched his head with his foot, they came to Toy Land where all the toys of the world are made by little dwarfs and fairies.

"Now I'll leave you," said the big Dream Bird, and he flew away, leaving little Mary Louise in front of a pretty shop full of Little Jack Rabbits, and, would you believe it, there was a toy Puss in Boots, Junior, with red top boots and a hat with a gold feather and a sword. And the workman who made these toys was a funny little dwarf with a green suit and a red cap and a long white beard.

"This is the land of wonderful toys

That are made for good little girls and boys,

Talking dolls and horses that run,

Everything here is made for fun,

But only good little girls and boys

Can have our wonderful, beautiful toys."

"Heigh ho," said Mary Louise, "what next, I wonder," and she looked at a toy regiment of wooden soldiers marching down the street.

Just then an old hand organ began to play,

"Oh, where are the songs of yesterday,

    And the songs we used to sing,

When you and I in the days gone by

    Danced in the Fairy's Ring?"

And up ran a little monkey dressed in a red coat and cap. Mary Louise gave him a penny, to hand to the old man who had stopped to set another tune to the organ.

"Over the hills and far away,

I've tramped all my life till I am gray,

And now with my organ and monkey clown

I find myself in little Toy Town,"

sang the old organ grinder as he sat down to rest with the little monkey on his lap.

"Are you very tired?" asked Mary Louise.

"Pretty tired," answered the old man. "All these years I've tramped and played, and now I find myself in a town where they make toys for children. But I see no children. Only playthings which I have no use for," and the old man sighed and patted the monkey and then he closed his eyes and fell asleep. And I guess he was very, very tired.

Then Mary Louise slipped away, out of Toy Town where the dwarfs and the fairies made all the toys in little workshops, only they had the shades pulled down so that nobody could see them, for they are queer little people and don't like to be watched.

"Oh, dear," sighed Mary Louise, "I wish I were home. Mother will be dreadfully worried about me.

"Oh, if I had a Wishing Stone

I know what I would do

I'd wish for lots of lovely things,

And give a lot to you.

But, Oh, dear me. I've never known

Where is this wonder Wishing Stone."

"I know," cried a little voice, and then, of course, Mary Louise looked all around to see who had spoken, but she couldn't see anybody.

"Who are you?" she asked, halting Dapple Gray on the edge of a big forest.

"Here I am," cried the same little voice, and then, quick as a wink, a tiny fairy jumped out from behind a bush.

"Don't frighten my pony," said Mary Louise, as Dapple Gray stood up straight on his hind legs, "he isn't used to fairies."

"No, indeed," whinnied the pony, for that is the way a horse talks, you know. "I've met lots of people in dear Old Mother Goose Land, but never a fairy."

"If you come into this forest you will meet many little people like me," answered the fairy.

"Will they object if I travel through it?" asked little Mary Louise anxiously. "You see, I'm on my way home."

"You have my permission," answered the fairy. "I'm queen of the Forest Fays. But I thought you were looking for the Wishing Stone?"

"Maybe I was," answered Mary Louise. "You see, I thought if I could find it, I'd wish I was home with my dear mother."

"It is not very far from here," said the little fairy. "Follow this path through the trees and by and by you'll come to it. But let me give you some advice. Be sure before you make your wish to say,

"Rose red, rose white,

I will try to do what's right."

"Thank you, I'll remember," answered little Mary Louise, and she turned Dapple Gray down the path to the woody glen.

Well, by and by, after a while, she saw a big white stone. It looked very like a rude stone chair, only of course, it didn't have any nice soft cushion in it like the one my grandmother used.

With a cry of joy little Mary Louise jumped from the saddle. "Now I'll make my wish!" And she sat down in the big stone chair and closed her eyes.

But, oh dear me. She had been in such a hurry that she forgot to say the little fairy verse and when she opened her eyes, there she was in the very same spot.

And, oh, dear me! again. Instead of the Dapple Gray, a little gray squirrel stood in the very spot where the little pony had been.

"If you would have what you would wish

   You must obey each rule,

No matter whether in your home

   Or in your Grammar School,"

sang a little yellow bird, as Mary Louise stared in amazement at the little gray squirrel.

"Oh, dear me," she sighed, "where is Dapple Gray?"

"I was your little pony,

And my name was Dapple Gray.

But now I am a squirrel

Because you did not say;

'Rose red, rose white,

I will try to do what's right,'"

answered the little squirrel.

And then Mary Louise remembered what the little fairy had told her to say when she made the wish. Oh, dear me. How sad she felt! But it was too late, and pretty soon the little squirrel ran away, and poor Mary Louise was left alone in the big Wishing Stone chair.

"Oh dear me," she sighed again, "now what shall I do?" But nobody answered, not even the little yellow bird, so she jumped down and started off through the wood, and by and by, after a mile, but never a smile, she heard somebody laughing. And, oh my, it was a great big, tremendous hearty laugh. Why, it made all the leaves tremble and the dry twigs fall to the ground. And then, all of a sudden, a giant walked by, carrying on his big finger the prettiest yellow bird you ever saw.

"Why bless my big leather belt," he exclaimed, "it's little Mary Louise."

"Oh, Mr. Giant," said Mary Louise, "I've disobeyed the Fairy Queen and lost my pony Dapple Gray."

"Bless my big hob-nailed club," said Mr. Merry Laugh, for this was the giant's name, "how did you come to do that?"

So Mary Louise told him how the Fairy Queen had directed her to the Wishing Stone, but that she had forgotten to say when making her wish,

"Rose red, rose white,

I will try to do what's right."

"Well, I'll give you another chance," said the big kind giant. "Now let me see," and he took off his big leather cap and scratched his head, and then he whispered something to the little yellow bird, but his whisper was so loud that of course Mary Louise heard it, for when a giant whispers it sounds like a man shouting, so I've been told.

"Come with me," said the giant after the little yellow bird had nodded her head, and pretty soon, not so very long, they came to his castle, where the giant made Mary Louise very comfortable in a little chair which had once belonged to his son.

"Now you rest here while I go and get out my big Gold Book," said Mr. Merry Laugh.

"Mr. Merry Laugh, the Giant,

 Has a big Gold Book,

Bound with leather hinges

 And a big brass hook,"

sang the little yellow bird.

"Now let me see," said the good, kind giant, opening the book and turning over the pages with his great immense thumb. "Ah, here it is," but before he began to read he took off his spectacles which were as big as automobile lamps and wiped them carefully on his red silk handkerchief which was bigger than a sail.

"Whoever disobeys the queen

 Can for his guilt atone

By making a little whistle

 Out of a turkey's bone."

"Ha, ha, ha!" roared the giant till the crystal chandelier tinkled like a million little bells and the portrait of his mother-in-law fell off the wall with a dreadful crash, "I never heard anything so funny before," and he picked up the portrait and laughed again, only this time even louder, for his mother-in-law's picture was all smashed to smithereens!

"Well, that's easy," he said after wiping his eyes. "Tomorrow will be Thanksgiving and you shall dine with me. And after dinner I'll give you a magic knife and if you can't make a whistle out of the drumstick bone, I'll have another portrait made of my mother-in-law."

"That's very good of you," said little Mary Louise.

"Don't mention it," replied the giant. "I have a book that once belonged to my boy when he was a little fellow. It's called the Iceberg Express, and you look so like the little girl on the cover that I'd almost believe you were she."

"I am, I am," shouted Mary Louise, jumping out of her chair. "And that's the reason I wanted to sit in the big Wishing Stone chair. I was going to wish I was home with mother."

"You don't say so," exclaimed Mr. Merry Laugh. "Well, well, well. It takes me back to the time when my boy was a little fellow and sat on my knee to hear me read Little Journeys to Happyland. How time flies!" And the big kind giant took his pocket handkerchief out again to wipe his blue eyes, and after that he went over to the piano and sang:

"If I had my little boy again

    How happy I should be,

I'd piggy-back him all around

    And trundle him on my knee.

"But oh, dear me. It's so long ago,

    And he's been away so long,

That all I can do is to wish and wish

    That he could hear this song."

"Dear me," said little Mary Louise, when the giant had finished. "You want your little boy and I want my mother."

Well pretty soon when Mary Louise walked into the dining room she saw the most wonderful turkey that ever graced a Thanksgiving table. Why, it weighed upty'leven pounds and was stuffed with a bushel of chestnuts.

"Now eat slowly and tuck your napkin under your chin," said Mr. Merry Laugh, "for we don't have Thanksgiving every day, although we ought to be thankful every day, just the same." And he stuck in the fork which was as big as a pitch-fork and began to carve with a knife that was even larger than General Pershing's sword.

Well, after a while, a mince pie was brought in, so large that it would have taken Mary Louise thirteen minutes to walk around it if the giant had placed it on the floor. But of course he didn't. No sireemam. He first cut a little piece for her and then a great big tremendous piece for himself, and would you believe he ate two pieces while she was eating one!

At last, when the dinner was over, and the giant had dried the wish bone on the steam heater till it was nice and dry, he handed little Mary Louise the magic knife and told her to make it into a whistle. And would you believe it if I didn't say so, in less than five hundred short seconds she had carved out the prettiest little whistle you ever saw.

"Now, little girl," said Mr. Merry Laugh, "blow on it and make a wish. But don't make the same wish you did before."

"Oh dear me," sighed the little girl. "I only wish one thing, and that is to be home with mother."

"Get your pony back and I'll help you," said Mr. Merry Laugh kindly.

So Mary Louise blew on her whistle and made a wish, when, all of a sudden, quicker than a wink, they heard a neigh in the courtyard, and looking out of the window, saw Dapple Gray.

"Here, take this little ring," said the giant, "and if ever you are in trouble, turn it around your finger three times and a half."

Just then the little yellow bird began to sing:

"'Tis a little golden ring,

Such a tiny, pretty thing.

But be careful lest you lose it,

For you may have need to use it,

It possesses such a charm

It will keep you from all harm."

"Good luck," said Mr. Merry Laugh as he opened the castle door. "Good-by and good luck. Drop in the next time you're in town, and don't forget Castle Merry Laugh, Forest City, U.S.A."

"Thank you," answered Mary Louise.

Just then down flew the beautiful Dream Bird.

"I'll take you home," he said. "Climb up between my wings!"

Then away he went through the air so softly that maybe the little girl fell asleep, for when she woke up, there she was on the beach where she had first met the little Mermaid Princess.

"Oh, oh," yawned Mary Louise, "am I really here?" But nobody answered, so she jumped to her feet and ran home to her mother.

Well, well, have we come to the end of the story, you and I, little reader? I'm sorry I've nothing more to tell you in this book, but listen—lean over to me and listen—I've written another book for the "Little Journeys to Happyland" series—it is called "The Wind Wagon." Isn't that a strange title? But I know you'll like it—yes, I'm sure you will.